The loom the weaver uses is called a backstrap loom. Portable and easy to construct,
backstrap looms date back to ancient history and are still used today. One end of the loom is
attached to a belt which the weaver wears around her back, and the other end is suspended
from a fixed object, commonly a tree, or, in the case of the loom in this book, a star.

Text copyright © 2010 by Thacher Hurd
Pictures copyright © 2010 by Elisa Kleven
All rights reserved
Distributed in Canada by D&M Publishers, Inc.
Color separations by Embassy Graphics
Printed in October 2009 in China by Toppan Leefung Printing Ltd.,
Dongguan City, Guangdong Province
Designed by Irene Metaxatos
First edition, 2010
1   3   5   7   9   10   8   6   4   2

www.fsgkidsbooks.com

Library of Congress Cataloging-in-Publication Data
Hurd, Thacher.
    The weaver / Thacher Hurd ; pictures by Elisa Kleven.— 1st ed.
        p.   cm.
    Summary: High above the world, a weaver spins thread from such things as clouds, dyes it with
colors from the sky and grass, and weaves a cloth filled with the emotions she sees throughout the
day to make a blanket of dreams.
    ISBN: 978-0-374-38254-4
    [1. Weaving—Fiction.   2. Dreams—Fiction.]   I. Kleven, Elisa, ill.   II. Title.

PZ7.H9562 Wed 2010
[E]—dc22
                                                                            2008028533

For Jan and Lee and Jordan
—J.H.

To Mollie, Dan, Loretta, Holly, Carl, and Jun
—E.K.

Beyond the earth,
near yet far,
the weaver sits
in the light of the rising sun,
singing a song,
watching the world,
while her fingers are at work.

First she spins her thread
from trails of shooting stars,
white clouds,
and spiderwebs hung with dew.

Then she dyes the thread
with the colors of the morning:
blue from the sky,
green from the grass,
yellow from the sun on the fields,
purple from the deep water.

As the sun rises high in the sky,
her fingers work faster,
and the shuttle begins to fly
back and forth
across her loom.

Looking down on the world,
the weaver sees
a smile on someone's face,

a hug between friends,
babies crying and then held warm
in their parents' arms,

children laughing,
a kiss given with love,
a heart that is full.

She weaves all these things
into her cloth:
a cloth of friendships,
loves intertwined—
happy,
sad,
angry,
joyful—
lives held together like vines.

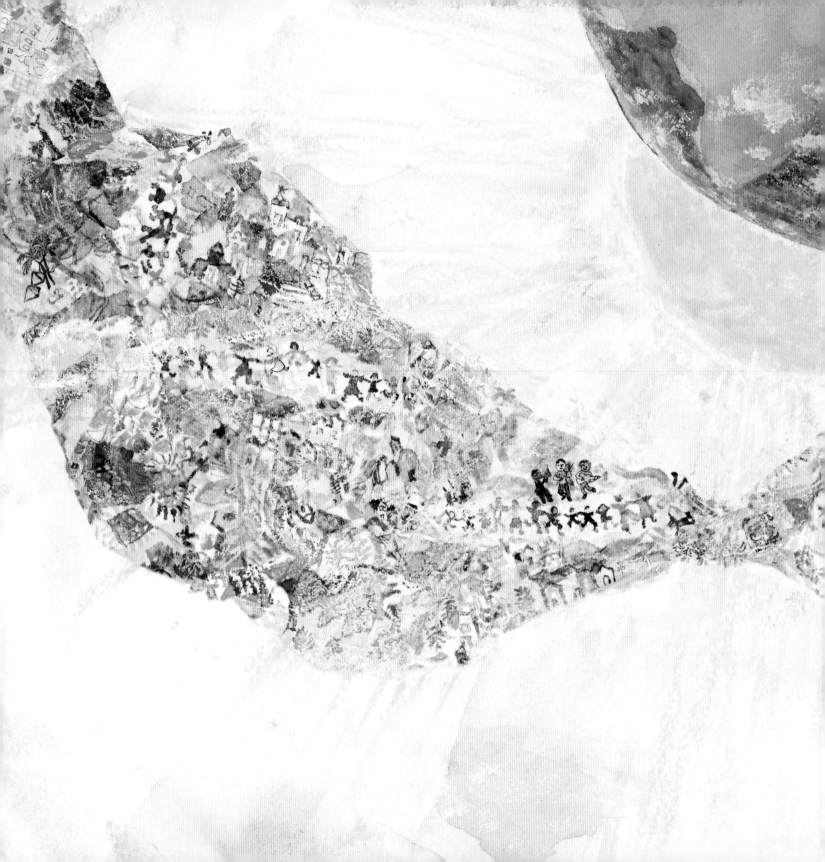

The sun is setting
and the weaver's work is almost done.
Gently she lifts the cloth from her loom
and begins to dance,

over mountains

and rivers and towns,

over cities and countries
and the deep ocean.

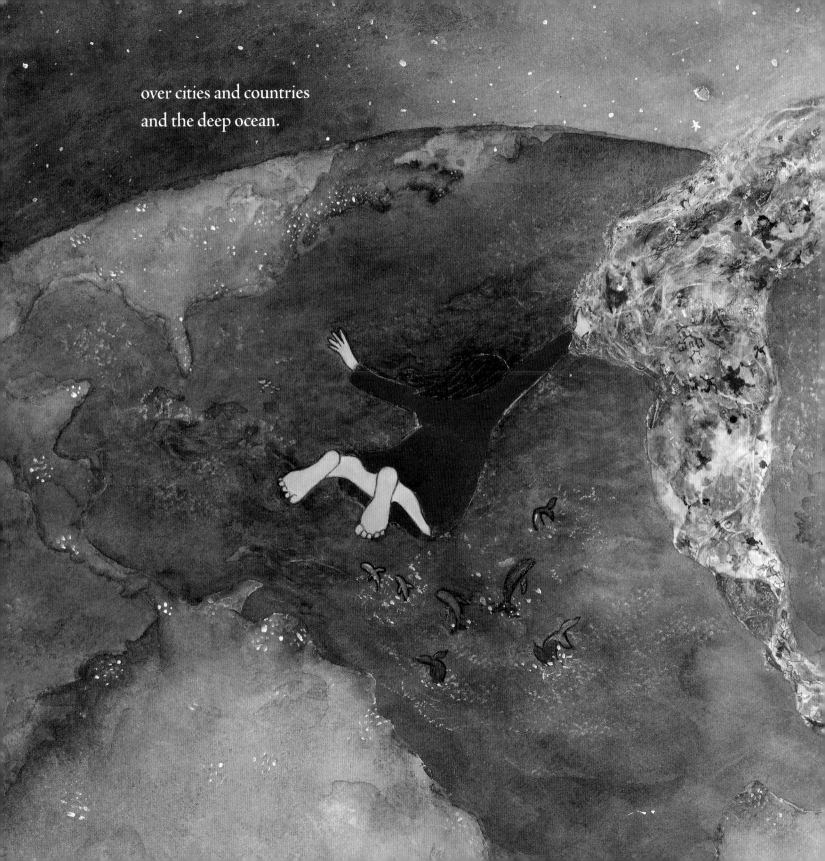

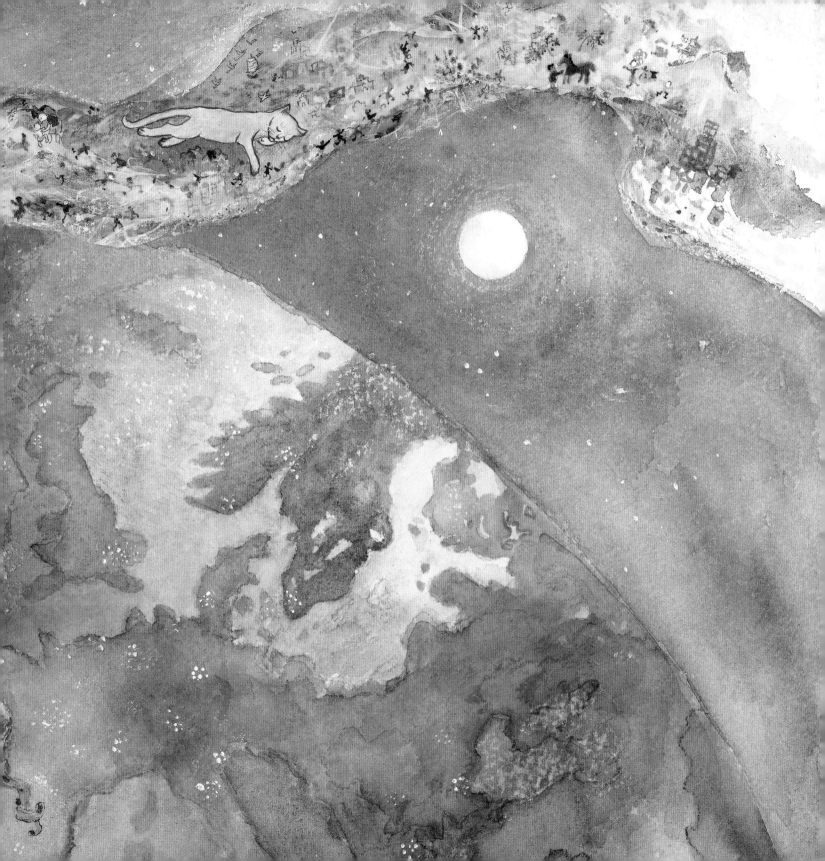

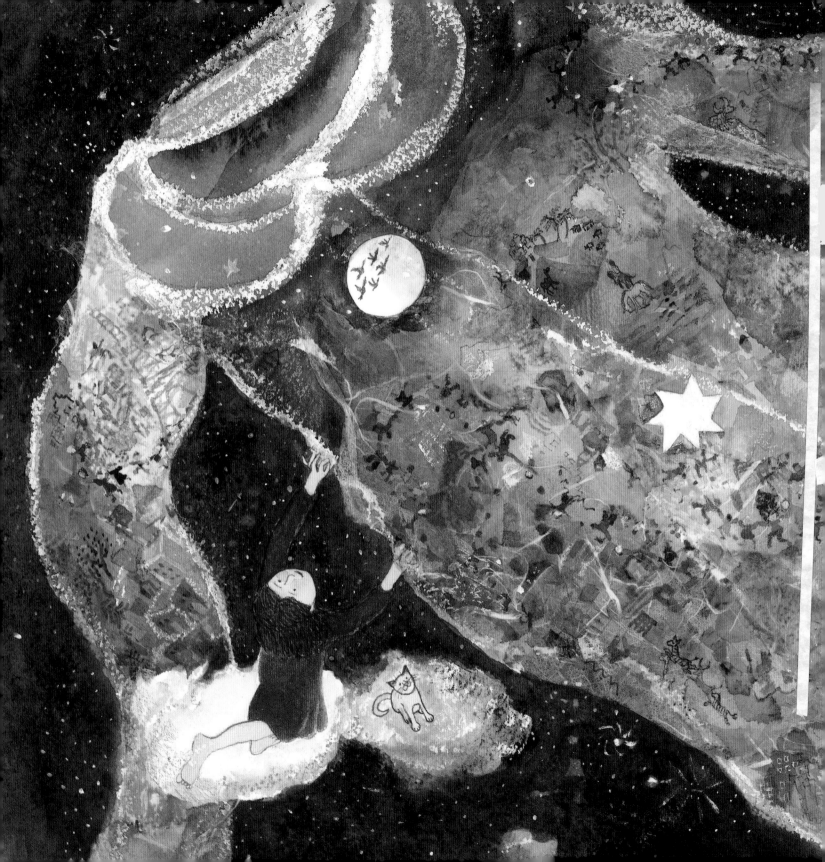

As she dances she spreads the cloth
like a coat across the night sky.
The stars and the moon are its buttons;
its pockets are filled with our memories.

It drifts down
to the earth below—
a coat to warm us
and protect us,
a coat to fill us with joy.
And as it settles around us
we dream in our beds,
while the moon glows above

and the weaver dances back to her home,

far above the world.